White
Spells
on
the G☉

About the Author

Originally from Cuba, Ileana Abrev now lives in Queensland, Australia, where she has her own spiritual practice and conducts workshops on magic, spirituality, meditation, chakras, and crystals. She has built a reputation for herself as a respected white witch among her customers and clients. With knowledge passed down to her from her father, an esteemed Santero, Ileana guides customers on a daily basis to solve problems with simple magic spells and positive visualization. She has been a practicing witch for over ten years.

White Spells on the Go

Ileana Abrev

Llewellyn Publications
Woodbury, Minnesota

First Edition
First Printing, 2009

Book design by Steffani Sawyer
Editing by Brett Fechheimer
Cover design by Lisa Novak
Cover art and interior illustrations © Mary Ross
Llewellyn is a registered trademark of Llewellyn Worldwide, Ltd.

Library of Congress Cataloging-in-Publication data for *White Spells on the Go* is pending.

ISBN: 978-0-7387-1449-3

Llewellyn Publications
A Division of Llewellyn Worldwide, Ltd.
2143 Wooddale Drive, Dept. 978-0-7387-1449-3
Woodbury, Minnesota 55125-2989, U.S.A.
www.llewellyn.com

Printed in the United States of America

Also by Ileana Abrev

Charm Spells
White Spells
White Spells for Protection
White Spells for Love

Dedicated to our ancestors,
for the gift and the know-how

Contents

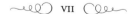

introduction

$\mathcal{R}$itual and magic governed every step, every thought, and every action of our ancestors' lives. Theirs was a time of worship, a time when festive seasons were named and celebrated according to planting and harvesting. But today, centuries later, ritual magic is long past its original heyday, and festivals are practiced symbolically by a faithful few. Yet there is something that lingers from ancestral generations, which is what I call "the essence": the essence of each individual family.

Each generation brings something sacred to the next: be it that secret recipe no one knows about, the blue eyes of your great-grandparents, the curly hair from your mother's side of the family, or the mannerisms of one of your parents. Not to mention your grandmother's advice, which I know you've taken or will someday take. I know I have, but mine was more on the magical, mystical side of things . . .

My family's generation gave me Santería, which is well known for its remedies. The smell of a lit cigar and the pungent, refreshing smell of Agua de Florida will always remind me of my youth, when I watched my father's guide, Francisco, give spiritual advice and counsel to my father's many clients with quick remedies.

I respect and hold Santería close to my heart, but I also love my Wiccan ways, so I combined Santería's remedies with my Wiccan beliefs and have created spells "on the go." Spells on the go are mini-spells that use earth-bound energies to cause an effect without a lengthy ritual. Earthbound energies can be anything from a crystal, an herb, or the flame of a candle, to the water from a stream, the earth on the ground, or the air that brushes through the meadows and fields.

I am compelled to share in this book my most intimate spells on the go, which I have used with positive results over the years. I have also shared them with others who sought my advice and guidance, only to be informed later of their own encouraging results. When I'm short on cash, I light a green candle. When I feel the negative energy of an unwanted entity, I burn frankincense incense in the house. When I need my partner to help me around the house—well, I just engrave his name with a pin on a red candle and light it, and I can assure you that this gets him off the couch. And if there is a time when I feel my guide is not by my side, I light a white candle and say, "Hey, come back here! I need you."

We live in a world of quick fixes. There is always a quick fix for something—a quick coffee, a quick bite to eat. Fast-food restaurants are first on our list for quick fixes; we even go to drive-through bank tellers because doing so is quicker than stopping and parking the car to make a deposit or a withdrawal.

We hardly have time for ourselves, much less our family or friends. We seem to make appointments left, right, and center just to catch up, go to dinner, or merely get together.

Most of us no longer experience the personal touch of a handwritten letter, but rather we receive cold e-mails on white-and-gray screens. With Internet dating, I guess love letters are a thing of the past, too. An impersonal text message can bring news of a job, a birth, or even a death. The intimate touch that once existed is long gone, now that "www" has come into our world.

Time is not going to stop for us, no matter how much we want it to slow down. We need to keep up with the fast pace of life in our magical workings, and we can achieve this with quick magical fixes for our everyday needs, using natural earthbound energies. I can honestly say you'll never look back.

There is no ritual behind spells on the go, but they do have visualizations; I can assure you that a positive visualization can make the universe do wonders. The universe

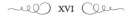 XVI

knows the fast pace we all live in, and it allows that fast pace in our magical workings, as does the Goddess. She always hears our cries for help—and if they're urgent, she's not going to say, "Hey, you need to do a ritual to dial my number," but instead she will say, "Let me see what I can do for you. I know you are in need."

By combining generations of magical know-how from Santería and Witchcraft, *spells on the go* are the only *way to go* in our fast-paced society. If we need to keep up to date with technology so that it doesn't pass us by, we need to do the same thing with magic. We cannot let generations of know-how pass into the history books just because there is no time for rituals. That is why, for anyone who wants to tap into magic, spells on the go are such a fresh concept.

Universal forces are always around us, and they are ready to listen to and act upon our desires and needs. You just need to make that connection with them—which might entail something as simple as lighting a white candle in order to take your message to the universe with the message "I need your help this day."

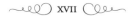 XVII

Have fun and enjoy *White Spells on the Go*, a book of spells for the modern world.

Blessed be,
Ileana

chapter 1

Earthbound and Universal Energies

$\mathcal{E}$arthbound energies take your message to the universe. They are not hard to find because they are all around us. You can touch them, feel them, smell them, and even hold them; you can bring earthbound energies into your world to manifest your deepest dreams and desires. These energies are anything that are nourished and grown by nature, such as herbs, crystals, and more.

Apart from earthbound energies, there is also a universal energy. Universal energy is of course the universe, and within the universe there are other energies, including the planets, the moon, the sun, the stars, and the homes of our most beloved deities and guides.

When both universal and earthbound energies are brought together to cause an effect, the impact is mind-boggling and the possibility of manifestation is endless. This is what I call "the birth of magic."

Most people associate magic with the occult; this is because magic is part of wizardry, fantasy, and is on the mystical and mythical side of things. But the good thing about magic is that it is interpreted in many different ways; religious faith and beliefs don't even come close. Magic is inexplicable, and to try to analyze or make sense of it is absolutely futile. So why try to make sense of it? Just accept it—once you do, you immediately believe that the unavailable is accessible. And who doesn't want that?

Believing is the key to receiving anything we want, and once you let earthly and universal energies into your everyday life, you will be opening the doors to one of the most accessible supermarkets in the world, a supermarket that only caters to your dreams. So why not shop for the things you want, need, or desire for your own spiritual or financial growth, or happiness?

 4

Once the correct energies are mixed together, then it is time to send them off to the universe for manifestation. This is done by using the art of positive visualization. The key to visualizing is to actually see what you want or desire in front of your mind's eye. Your visualization must be as clear as watching a television show. Once you've done this, then it is time to sit and wait patiently for what you've asked for, but you must always keep your desires in mind, see them, and believe in them.

The first rule of spellcasting is to always stay positive, no matter the odds or the conditioning of your mind. If you say something is going to work, it will work—and this attitude you should always have, not only with magic but with everything else you do in life.

The tool stash

There is no right or wrong way to start your spells on the go, and this is because they are simple and there are no lengthy rituals behind them. But there may be a time

when a day of the week or a certain moon phase will be needed to enhance the spell.

To start off with, you may want to stock up on a few items and keep them all together for easy access, such as:

- Different-colored ribbons and cloths

  You will be using them at times to enhance the needs you wish to manifest. Make sure the ribbons are all cotton.

- Candle holders

  These do not have to be expensive, just durable.

- Colored candles

  The candles need to be true to their color, which means that if they are blue on the outside, they will need to be blue on the inside as well. You don't want to confuse the universe when you are making your intentions known.

- Crystals

  Try to obtain a small variety of crystals. The main ones you want to buy are amethyst and clear quartz.

- Essential oils and an oil burner

    An oil burner is not only used for aromatherapy for medicinal purposes or to alleviate stress; it can also be used in magic. Essential oils are also often used in magical workings. An oil burner is usually ceramic, but the type of oil burner you choose is up to you. You may even have one already!

- Drawstring bags

    You can purchase or make drawstring bags. Making them is simple. Just cut a square piece of material, its color depending on the actual spell. Then make a little bag out of the material and keep it closed so that its contents don't fall out.

- Herbs

    You can find herbs just about anywhere. Try the supermarket first. Then, if you can't find a particular herb, go to a nursery or your friendly New Age store, where the employees will be able to help you. If you can only find fresh herbs, that's okay, but you need to dry them unless the spell specifies to use them fresh. To dry them, lay them flat in a shaded area on a piece of a brown paper bag for a few days until the leaves are crunchy to the touch.

• Censer and charcoal tablets

You can use a small bowl for your censer or a tiny cauldron with three legs. It does not matter if it is metal or glass. You can just burn dry herbs on their own by lighting a match to the dry herbs, but if you want to get more out of your dry herbs or resins, just fill the bottom of the censer with either dirt or sand, even rock salt, to insulate the container, and then place a charcoal tablet on top. It's better to light it outside the house, since it initially gives off a not-so-pleasing gray smoke. Then, when it becomes red-hot, you can add your herbs on the top of the charcoal. Be aware that the charcoal tablets are a fire hazard and should be treated with care. Do not drop them on the floor or use them around small children—the burns are very painful.

These are just a few of the tools that you will need to conduct spells on the go. Once you get to know the spells and do them, it will be easy to replenish your tool stash so that you'll always have the things you need at your fingertips at a minute's notice.

chapter 2

Days of the Week and Planets

We take the days of the week for granted. We mainly associate them with our daily schedules. We think about Monday, Tuesday, Wednesday, Thursday, and Friday as working days, chore days, and school days. Saturdays are the days we spend doing the things we didn't have time to do during the week, and Sunday is the day we basically catch up with family, friends, movies, or even the book we're reading.

The days of the week are closely associated with the planets, and our ancestors used them to capture the planets' essences into their magical and healing rituals. We can do the same because these are universal energies that have been around since the inception of all that we have ever known. Each planet has a close association to a day of the week.

You can use the days of the week with the planets to conduct spells. The planets and the days of the week are such powerful energies that they convey to the universe our needs and desires. For example, if you are doing a money spell, you may want to do it on a Thursday, which is the day for financial gain and wealth. Love spells are best conducted on Fridays, since Friday is associated with Venus, the goddess of love.

Days of the week and planets on the go

Sunday—Sun

The sun is the bright star at the center of our solar system. Its day is Sunday, and you can use this powerful energy, along with your creativity, in anything you wish to accomplish. Sunday is a great day to do a spell to sell your home or a business, or to buy a house or a car. This is also a great day to communicate with your spiritual guides. The sun gives hope when there is none to be found.

Monday—Moon

Monday is the day of our beloved moon, and this is a day when anything is possible. If you don't know what day to do a spell, do it on a Monday. The moon is filled with emotion and love. On this day we can conduct healing spells. You can also use this day to listen to your gut feelings and make serious decisions. You can use your psychic abilities to see into the future on a Monday.

Tuesday—Mars

Tuesday is filled with confidence. This is due to the influence of Mars, which is very masculine and full of determination. We can use Tuesdays for protection, working against negative forces, and getting rid of bad spirits or anything else that is bad for us. Tuesday is also a day for getting things done or for finishing an overdue project.

Wednesday—Mercury

We all know Wednesday as "hump day," the middle of the working week. This is an excellent day to conduct business spells. Mercury helps with any type of family communication or in discussions with adversaries. Wednesdays are for winning arguments, or for making travel arrangements and wishing for a vacation. Mercury helps others say what they actually want or mean; if you want to know if someone loves you, this is the day to conduct spells for a truthful answer in order to help others see your point of view.

Thursday—Jupiter

Jupiter is the biggest planet in our solar system, and for this reason I use Thursdays for my money needs. You can use Thursdays to conduct wishing spells, luck spells, and abundance spells. Jupiter can be used for working on relationships or to find a happy medium during disagreements. You can also use Jupiter to conduct calming anger spells and addiction spells.

Friday—Venus

Friday is Venus, and she is the goddess of love. This is a time for love spells. On Fridays you can do attraction spells, friendship spells, work on your sexuality, and bring things out into the open. The best love spells are done on Fridays with a full moon. On this day, Venus gets ready to party and you should do the same. Venus and Friday bring pleasure to our world.

Saturday—Saturn

Saturday is a day for magical discipline. If you are true to your faith, this is the day to let the universe know. On Saturdays, you will be conducting protection spells and spells to get rid of negative energies. Saturday is the planning day. Saturn is very strict and stubborn, and this is why negative energy spells should be conducted on this day, because Saturn gives you the determination to stay focused. Saturday is a day to break free from a bad love affair or a person who doesn't take no for an answer. Hold Saturday close to your heart; for protection, Saturday is your day.

chapter 3

Color

The importance of color in our lives is well known. We need color, and without color our lives would be very bland indeed. Color is part of our everyday lives, and the colors of our clothes are at the top of the list. Every morning we decide what to put on. Some days we like a certain outfit, but on other days that same outfit may not appeal to us. This is because of the energy we unconsciously put out. We don't realize it, but our bodies scream for a certain color—and they let us know this by making that color attractive to our eyes.

Some colors, like red and orange, give out strong vibrations of warmth. Other colors, such as pink and light blue, give out passive vibrations that are soothing to the soul. Even many doctors have opted to swap their clinical white coats for blue ones, a move that has proven to lessen patients' fears and even their blood pressure.

Also, and most important, color enhances the needs we want to convey to the universe. Color is an essential part of magic and should always be consulted. Each color has a powerful meaning, and this meaning enhances our magical needs—not to mention our psychological and healing needs.

I use color on a daily basis. When I feel that I need protection, I wear black. When I feel down, I wear red to help lift myself up. When I need money, I strap a green cotton band around my wrist and shout to the universe that I'm in need. Green is the universal color for money, since it represents growth and prosperity. I'm immediately in tune with universal forces because of the green band around my wrist, which colors my entire etheric field like a green light bulb and acts as a beacon, sending my needs to the universe.

I've found that color bands are an easy way to make my magical needs known. They are also easy to create. Just cut some cotton material in the color of your needs and wrap this material around your right wrist (or around your left wrist if you are left-handed). Wrap this material around your wrist three times, and each time say your needs out loud to the universe, visualize them like a television commercial, and then make a knot to keep the band in place. Don't take the band, or bands, off until you feel your needs are being satisfied; make your color bands pleasing to the eye, as you may have to wear them for a few days.

Color bands on the go

To find peace: Light-blue band

To heal illness: White band

For luck, money, and growth: Green band

To heal the heart: Dark-pink band

To enhance learning and studying: Yellow or orange band

For strength: Orange or red band

Love: Pink band

To combat negativity: Black or red band

To avoid stress: Blue band

Protection: Black band and a red band

To work against depression: Red band and an orange band

Fertility: Orange, but wrap it around your waist only one time

To fight sadness: Blue and pink bands wrapped together

Attraction: Red—but don't tie a knot, just a simple bow

Soul connection: Lavender band

Psychic workings: Purple bands around both wrists

To deal with anger: Light-blue band

Communication with angels: Gold band

To listen to your gut feelings: Yellow band

Women's health issues: Orange band

Before exams: Bright yellow band

Astral travel: Purple band and a white band

To calm down a very active toddler: Light-blue band

For a job interview: Orange band and a blue band together, but don't wear them—just stick them in your pants or jacket pocket.

To enhance the chakras: Get red, orange, yellow, green, blue, purple, and pink ribbons and make a plait out of them all. Once you've done this, wrap it around your wrist like a bracelet, and your chakras will always be in tune to your needs.

Protection for babies: For both girl and boy babies, tie a red ribbon to a safety pin and fasten it to the baby's clothes where no one can see it.

Overall magical colors

- **White:** Healing
- **Yellow:** Psychic abilities
- **Red:** Courage and strength

- **Purple:** Communication and peace
- **Blue:** Protection and calm
- **Pink:** Love and relationships
- **Black:** Protection against negative forces
- **Green:** Healing, money, and spiritual growth

chapter 4

Crystals

*C*rystals are precious and extremely beautiful. They have aided our ancestors spiritually and physically for millennia. Once you tap into a crystal's unique beauty and strength, the effect is transformational. When worn or carried, crystals transmit a feeling of peace. Like a candle in the mist of darkness, a sense of spiritual enlightenment warms the heart. Anger becomes a thing of the past, and you exude love and compassion to those around you.

Today, the legacy of crystals is stronger than ever before. Crystals are a wonderful complementary tool in magic. The energies within each individual crystal work in unison with each individual. When the energy of a crystal merges with your own, sparks take to the air and those sparks take your wishes and needs to the universe.

Crystals absorb as well as project energy, which means that lots of other people may have handled your crystal and imbued it with their own energy before you did. For that reason, it's important to cleanse your crystal before you program it with your intent. There are many ways to cleanse a crystal, with no right or wrong way to do so—I will guide you through this process. If a spell in this section does not indicate a cleansing method, you still need to cleanse your crystal, which you can do by placing it in a glass of water and adding a large spoonful of salt. Mix the salt with the water and crystal, and leave the mixture outside for one night in your backyard or on a balcony before doing the spell.

The effects of crystals are wide and varied, but in general they are potent protective and healing talismans that can transform your life in any way you want them to, providing you have the desire to change, the will to believe, and you forever hold the love and understanding the crystals will bring.

Crystals on the go

Accidents

A carnelian agate is best. Just rinse this crystal with some rainwater, hold it in your hands, and visualize prevention where you need it the most. Keep the crystal with you at all times.

Aggression

For those who share their unwanted aggression with you, keep a bloodstone crystal close to your heart at all times and the aggressor will no longer be aggressive.

Alcoholism

If you want to stop drinking, cleanse an amethyst crystal deep within the earth for an entire day. Then keep this very powerful crystal with you at all times. Every day, visualize that you dislike drinking alcohol until you actually do, and your addiction will diminish.

Angels

When you seek the guidance of an angel, hold a clear quartz crystal close to your heart and ask for divine direction and you shall find it.

Anger

When you want to calm someone's unnecessary anger, leave a blue-lace agate crystal out on the grass on a full-moon night. The next morning, hold this crystal in your hands and visualize this person's anger subsiding and as a thing of the past. Then hide the crystal where it will never be found by the one who needs calming down.

Anxiety

The jitters of anxiety can be quieted down by wearing a pyrite crystal. Cleanse this crystal with a drop of lavender essential oil, and as you do so, visualize that which gives you anxiety. Hang this crystal from your neck, and every time you are anxious, touch the crystal with your index finger. Feel the calming, soothing sensations that only pyrite can give running through your body.

Asthma

Always wear a rose quartz crystal for your asthma, or have one under your pillow.

Aura

To strengthen your aura, hold a clear quartz crystal and it will magnify your aura tenfold.

Bad temper

For those who would rather fight than talk, place amethyst and blue agate crystals under their pillows.

Broken heart

To heal a broken heart, place a rose quartz crystal on top of a grassy patch and leave it out all night. Carry this crystal close to your heart at all times, and it will heal the pain you are suffering deep down inside.

Cancer

For those who suffer from cancer, a smoky quartz and an amethyst crystal should always be worn. The quartz heals while the amethyst pacifies. This will aid and strengthen your faith while treatment is being conducted and remission is at hand.

Children

The best crystal for children to have is a tiger-eye. Cleanse it with baby oil and hold it in your hands, while visualizing the protection and growth you wish for your children. Then place this crystal in the children's room, where it cannot be found by them.

Clarity of mind

When the mind is boggled with problems, hold an aquamarine crystal in your hands, and as you do so, visualize your mind clear, with your problems solved and with no more worries.

Clairvoyance

To aid spiritual workings, have in front of you a lapiz lazuli or a ruby crystal. These two crystals take the mind further than any other.

Confidence / Courage

If it's confidence you need, then it's confidence you shall have. Cleanse an onyx crystal under the sun for an hour. Then, while it is still hot in your hands, visualize the confidence you need and you will have it.

Creative expression

If you need creativity, carry with you a bloodstone crystal.

Danger

If you feel danger is ahead, carry with you a malachite crystal.

Depression

Depression can bring you down, but a kunzite crystal will help to lift you up.

Dreams

For total dream recall, cleanse an azurite crystal with lavender water and always have it under your pillow. Think of your dreams before you get out of bed, as that way they will stay longer in your mind for you to analyze them.

Energy

If it's energy you're lacking, wear as much silver jewelry as you can. Silver is a conductor of energy, and it will give you plenty.

Enemies / Envy

For the enemies and envy in your office, put a tiger-eye crystal on your desk. It will repel those enemies you don't need to have, and the envious ones will go away.

Evil eye

I know of only one crystal that can protect you from the evil eye, and that is tiger-eye when it is worn.

Faithfulness

For a faithful partner, place a blue agate crystal under your partner's pillow.

Fertility / Pregnancy

To become pregnant, carry a tiger-eye, carnelian agate, and a red jasper crystal with you at all times. To have a healthy pregnancy, carry a howlite crystal inside your bra.

Financial stability / Fortune

To keep that financial stability going, wear opals or carry a bloodstone crystal in your purse or wallet.

Friends

To keep and make friends, a bloodstone crystal should do the trick.

Happiness

Keep together a moonstone and a moss agate crystal in a little orange drawstring bag, and it will make you happy with every beat of your heart.

Headaches / Migraines

Stress headaches can be avoided if you cleanse a hematite crystal and wear it as a necklace.

Hope

When you think hope has gone, find a citrine crystal and keep it in your pocket, but not before you cleanse it with a drop of bergamot, which is the "happy" essential oil.

Intellect / Intuition

A rhodochrosite crystal that has been cleansed in rainwater and worn around the neck will boost the intuition and intellect.

Jealousy

Without a jealous partner knowing, place under his or her pillow an apophyllite crystal, and there will be nothing for your partner to feel jealous about.

Love

For self-love, the best crystal to have is a rose quartz.

Lover

A tiger-eye crystal exchanged between lovers will aid with the future of what is yet to come.

Luck

There is no such thing as bad luck when you carry a tiger-eye crystal.

Meditation

When meditating, it is always good to hold a crystal in your hand; that crystal should always be a clear quartz or an amethyst crystal.

Memory

Some days you may not remember the color of your underwear, so carry a fluorite crystal—and you'll remember not just the color of your underwear but also the brand name.

Menopause

If you think you are near the crone years, carry with you a ruby crystal and keep it close to your heart.

Money

Over the years, I have discovered that the money-attracting crystals are citrine and red jasper. The citrine brings abundance, and the red jasper attracts new work opportunities that bring in the cash.

Negative energies

To combat the negative energies of unwanted entities, cleanse a tiger-eye and an apache-tear crystal in a glass of water with a teaspoon of rock salt. Leave this mixture outside on a full-moon night, and on the third day bring it inside. Now hold the crystals in your hands and visualize the negative energy you want to ward away. Carry the crystals with you every day.

Peace

We all want a peaceful home, free of arguments. A rose crystal and an amethyst quartz crystal will do the job. To keep the energy flowing, keep the crystals where your family congregates.

Protection

For the protection of the self, always carry a tiger-eye crystal.

Psychic abilities

To magnify your psychic abilities, always have with you a lapis lazuli crystal.

Sadness

When there is sadness in your heart due to a breakup or because you've lost a loved one, hold or carry an amethyst crystal in your hand, and the pain will lessen every day.

Sleep

If you're unable to sleep, keep an amethyst crystal in a sock under your pillow, and add to it a drop of lavender essential oil. You will then be able to sleep all night without looking at the clock.

Strength

If you need the personal strength to face situations that seem uneven, drop an aquamarine crystal in a glass. Keep it out where the moonlight shines at night, and in the morning drink the water—but please don't swallow the crystal!

Stress

To fight stress, the best remedy is to hang a moonstone crystal around your neck 24/7. The stress will go away, but if it ever returns, again hang a moonstone crystal around your neck at all times.

Verbal expression

The best crystal to hold in your hand when you need to express yourself is an aquamarine crystal; it will never let you down when you need to make a point.

Violence

If you ever suffer from violent abuse, carry with you a bloodstone crystal, and you will seek the help you need to be able to walk away.

Magical crystals for the home

Clear quartz protects your home and your loved ones from unwanted negative energies.

Amethyst is calming and soothing. It brings peaceful and calming energies to the home. It helps those who have a little bit of a temper, and it brings relief to those who suffer from stress.

Citrine can bring abundance to the home, whether it be an abundance of love, happiness, and/or money. When worn, it can also help the young ones to retain the information they learn in school. Citrine also helps its wearers find the patience they need to confront uncomfortable situations.

Agates come in all colors and can bring out the courage necessary to stand up for yourself. Pink agate is for love; green agate is for money; brown agate is good for those who are trying to quit an addiction to something, such as cigarettes or alcohol; and blue agate is for healing. Agate is one of those crystals that you should always have in your home.

Rose quartz can help us find love, but it can also help us love ourselves above all—because if we don't love who we are, then no one else will. Like amethyst, rose quartz can calm the beast in all of us if we place it under the pillow before bedtime.

Remember that crystals are a gift from nature. It is said that if everyone in the world wears or has a crystal in the home, the earth will regenerate from all we have taken away from her. If you are asking yourself, "Is this true?" —well, I certainly don't doubt it!

 43

Crystals for each day of the week

Sunday: To heal the self and learn something new, use a citrine crystal

Monday: To find purity and protection in your life, use a clear quartz crystal

Tuesday: For strength and passion all the way, use a garnet crystal

Wednesday: To find wisdom and togetherness without the stress, use an amethyst crystal

Thursday: To find patience and tranquillity, use a sodalite crystal

Friday: For the growth of love in your life, use an aventurine crystal

Saturday: To rid all the week's negativity and to stay positive for the week ahead, use an onyx crystal

chapter 5

All That Grows

$\mathcal{E}$verything on this earth vibrates with beautiful, uninhibited forces. These innocent but strong, willful energies are found anywhere. Anything that is green and growing is filled with a strong sense of wisdom and strength. This wisdom and strength can be utilized to grow and prosper on a spiritual level. These energies can be anything from the bark of a tree to the grass under your feet; just because they can't talk, it doesn't mean they are dead or unworthy. On the contrary, they are very much alive, and believe it or not, they are waiting for us to seek their aid.

Some laugh at those who talk to plants as though they were people. But it has been proven that this interaction with plants has positive results, and more people are doing it; some people even sing and play music to plants.

I sometimes get a few stares when I hug a tree on my daily walks with nature, but I can't help it—hugging trees makes me feel good. From strong, healthy trees I seek energy and wisdom, and for the ones that look a bit sad, I pass on healing energies through my touch. This is a wonderful experience. I'm not only out with nature, but I certainly feel a part of it.

Everything that is green falls into this wonderful category: plants, trees, herbs, and even flowers have a special purpose for their existence. Our ancestors knew this truth and they have passed it down to us—not just for medicinal needs but for magical needs as well. For example, not only did they use chamomile for colic, fevers, indigestion, and as a hair rinse to bring the natural highlights out, but they also used chamomile's magical powers in love baths and in protection and purifying sachets.

I always have fresh basil and rosemary in my house. I make arrangements out of these herbs soon after I pick them from my garden. Rosemary is good for cooking as well as protection, and basil keeps the finances healthy and protected! These strong, powerful herbs can do no wrong, but you don't need to blend them together; each one has its own special qualities and works rather well on its own to bring a much needed effect or change. I just like putting them together, and their scent really purifies my home.

In magic, all that is green is used to its fullest. We crush, burn, and dry everything for a purpose. We crush to blend, we burn to purify, and we can even dry all that is green to place in little drawstring bags for a specific purpose.

We are going to use these wonderful energies, and use them to their highest potential to enhance the needs and wants we hope to achieve. Let's do the quick fixes by visualizing our needs, and making them happen by using a little bit of this and a little bit of that!

Herbs for protection on the go
Protect your home from unwanted entities
Sprinkle angelica all over the house on Saturday before sundown, and unwanted entities will no longer want to visit.

Keep thieves away

To ward away thieves, hang from your back door a little red drawstring bag and fill it up with caraway seeds. But be sensible: always lock your front door and back door when you're not home.

Vacations

To stay safe while you're on vacation, take a cotton ball and soak it in witch hazel oil. Rub the cotton ball filled with the oil inside the shoes you will be wearing most often on your trip. Leave your shoes out on a full-moon night and seek protection from the moon and its light.

It's best to do this on a Saturday, and protected you will be during your vacation.

Protect your home from outside negative forces

When you are ready to mop your floors, add to the bucket a teaspoon of cumin powder and a tablespoon of rock salt; as you mop, visualize the protection you seek for your home.

Protection against gossip

In a little black drawstring bag, place a small handful of uncooked rice and a bunch of fresh rosemary leaves. Hold this little bag in your hand and visualize the gossip not getting near you. See it fading away like smoke.

Uninvited guests

Behind your front door, always have a large head of garlic. Anyone who wants to come in without an invitation will think twice before crossing the threshold.

Protection for your children

Under your children's pillows, place a laurel leaf and visualize the protection you feel they need. Or get some fennel, crush it in a mortar and pestle, and sprinkle it in their shoes. Protected they will be without even knowing it.

Fresh protection

Make a bunch of herbal arrangements every Saturday. In a vase full of water, add rosemary, basil, parsley, and mint. Within this arrangement, place a few leaves from a fern to make it look good. Keep this arrangement on the center table of your living room. Protected you will be, and don't forget to refresh the arrangement every week.

Herbs for love on the go

To attract the love you want

Eat an apple and pick out the seeds. Place the seeds on a white cloth and let them dry in a shaded area until they desiccate. Sprinkle lavender talcum powder on them and keep them under your pillow to attract the love you've always wanted.

To be loved

Take all the petals from a dry red rose and a dry white rose and mix the petals together. Add a dash of cinnamon and a star anise. Mix this all together and place it in a small pink box with a handwritten note that says you will be loved forevermore. Sign your name to the note and close the box.

For attraction

Carry with you three vanilla beans! And attractive to others you will be.

To heal a broken heart

Find an elm tree and wrap your arms around it. Wish it to heal your broken heart, and leave behind a coin on the ground as a healing payment.

To spice up the marriage bed

Crush patchouli and dill together. Two hours before bed, sprinkle this powder on the sheets. Wait and see, and the fun you seek will be.

For a night on the town

Before you go out on the town, sprinkle cinnamon inside your shoes. They will take you where the fun is and to the people you want to meet.

To find love

Always have with you a myrtle leaf inside your bosom.

To keep love

To keep the love you have, tie together two sandal-wood sticks with a red ribbon and place them under the middle of your mattress.

To find out if someone is in love with you

Write the full name of the person on a piece of paper. Cover the paper with a whole bunch of chestnuts, and that person will tell you yes or no.

To send a love letter

After you have written your love letter, sprinkle lavender leaves on it and let the leaves sit on top of the paper for a day or so. Make sure your mind has nothing but love thoughts for the person for whom the letter was intended. Take the piece of paper outside and blow the lavender in the direction of the wind; then fold the letter, mail it, and you will see.

Herbs for luck and money on the go

For a lucky home

Have lots of violet plants in your home.

To have money in your purse or wallet

Sprinkle nutmeg between the bills and it will just multiply them evenly.

For wealth

Have a bowl of pecans by the front door but don't eat them; if you do eat them, you will be eating your financial needs.

For luck

Carry with you a lucky hand root, and lucky you will be in all you do.

To make a business fruitful

Behind your business door always have a bowl of sesame seeds, and on top of them sprinkle a little bit of gold-dust powder.

To have success in life

For success, carry with you a piece of a ginger root and replace it with a new one every month and a day.

Money pillow

Make a little pillow with green cotton material and fill it up with Irish moss. Carry it with you at all times for your money needs.

To win the lottery

Put it out there that you want to win the lottery jackpot. Mix together ginger, nutmeg, and sage. Sprinkle the mixture on top of your lottery ticket and put your ticket high up, in a safe place, until the night of the drawing. Do this every time you dream about winning!

Nuts we are!

Always have out a bowl filled with mixed nuts. Every morning before you leave the house, take a nut with you for luck and, at the end of the day, leave it at the front door of your bank.

Coin jar

Keep a jar filled with coins and add to it saffron powder from the supermarket. The jar will keep multiplying the coins.

Pinecones

Hang from your key ring a small pinecone, and every morning dip it in rosemary leaves for your money and luck needs.

chapter 6

Incense

hen I was young, and even to this day, my mother smoked out her house with rosemary leaves. She would take three or four barbecue charcoals and place them on the stove, waiting until each charcoal was blood-red. Then she picked up the charcoals with a pair of kitchen tongs, placed them in a silver baking dish, and added a handful of rosemary leaves. She took this very powerful, blinding smoke all around the house. Well, she used to do so before my sister and I introduced her to the charcoal tablet, a much easier and safer way to purify the house, but some habits are hard to break. She still likes the old way better, and when she doesn't have any charcoal tablets, she goes back to her old ways quite happily.

There is the type of incense that is store-bought, and then there are the types of incense you make yourself. I can honestly say that I use both kinds. I use store-bought incense for its fragrance; for a particular scent on its own—like rose, lavender, or patchouli—I just light it up with the thought in mind of what my needs are, and the incense works rather well along with positive visualization.

Now, the make-it-yourself type of incense is always the best. I believe the more smoke you make, the more energy you put out (maybe this is an inherited trait!), but please don't trigger the smoke detectors like I've done in the past!

Incense smoke is one of the quickest ways to let the universe know your needs, and that's why I use it for quick fixes in spells on the go. The air element holds your wish in a bubble of smoke and directs it where you want it to go. You only need the actual dry herb (unless otherwise specified), the charcoal tablet in a censer, and your needs.

You can burn herbs or coarse resins like frankincense tear drops, myrrh, or dragon's blood, which are very powerful when working with negative forces.

For the perfect outcome, combine these energies with the days of the week in order to bring, luck, riches, peace, harmony, and love—not to mention the purification effects they produce when you are using them for healing, psychic work, or even to get rid of a negative entity or energy. So, the next time you see an incense stick, remember that it is much more than just an aromatic fragrance!

Smoke on the go

House cleansing: Rosemary

Close all your doors and windows, but leave the front door open. Take this smoke throughout the house, going from the back to the front door. As soon as you finish, you will feel sparkling and new refreshing energies.

Self-cleansing: Frankincense tears

Place your charcoal tablet in its censer with two frankincense tears and then place it on the floor. Stand naked in front of it and let the smoke engulf your body. Feel all the negativity inside of you leaving your body, to be replaced by only good energies.

Protection: Dragon's blood

Burn dragon's blood in your censer once a week for the protection of your home.

Peace: Lavender

Lavender leaves on a charcoal tablet will keep your home peaceful, as well as all of those within its walls.

Negative energies: Rue

If you can tolerate the smell of dry rue on top of a hot charcoal tablet, you can tolerate anything—but negative energies hate it, which is why I use it.

Love: Rose petals

Unfortunately, the scent of burning dry rose petals is not as pleasant as you would think, but if you mix them in a mortar and pestle with rosemary leaves, you will have a very tolerable and powerful love smoke that you may want to take to the bathroom with you while you have a bath. As you bathe, think only of the love you wish to have in your life.

Creating good energies: Myrrh

Myrrh is quite pleasant to the nose. Take your censer all around your home in a counterclockwise motion, and as you do, you will create good energies.

Removing an unwanted entity: Thistle

Burn this herb in the area where you believe the entity is and yell out to it three times as the thistle burns: "Get out, get out, get out of my home and life!"

Healing: Sandalwood and frankincense

Sprinkle sandalwood on top of your charcoal tablet, and then add one tear of frankincense. Meditate on the healing you wish and visualize the smoke going toward the one in need.

Money: Basil and parsley

Crush together dry parsley and basil and then burn the mixture once a week, using the days of the week and planets; your money needs will be answered.

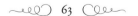

Good luck: Nutmeg and cinnamon

From your spice rack at home, mix together half a teaspoon of nutmeg and cinnamon. The combination may smell like the festive season, but the luck it brings will always be in season!

Hex breaking: Angelica and cloves

Visualize the hex you would like to break. Then place three cooking cloves and a dash of angelica on top of the charcoal. See the hex breaking like a piece of glass on a tile floor. Repeat every day for three days.

chapter 7

The Scents of Oils

The magic of oils was part of our ancestors' lives, and we can honor them by incorporating oils into our quick magical fixes. I've always had good results with essential oils. I keep all my little bottles of oils in a cedar box, which absorbs each and every single one of their mystical and magical scents. When I take out this box, my entire house is bewitched by the energies of the oils and their powerful fragrances, which automatically lets me know that I'm ready to start my magical workings.

Essential oils are derived from aromatic plants, which are processed to produce a particular oil. This oil is as pure as it gets and vibrates with earthbound energies. These aromatic oils are alive and filled with magical properties even after the distillation process.

People are becoming more aware of the healing and relaxing properties of oils by way of aromatherapy and invigorating massages that leave them feeling totally relaxed and re-energized. Just as you need real essential oils for these types of therapies, you also need the real deal when using essential oils for magic. Synthetics just don't cut it!

Each one of these oils has its own properties, just as herbs do. These oils are so powerful that, with just a single drop, you can send your magical needs to the universe loud and clear. But be careful: some people are allergic to oils because of the strength they possess. I've known people to be allergic to the scent of pure lavender oil. These folks get sick to their stomachs because lavender oil can be so sickly sweet. A single drop can linger for hours in an oil burner. So take care when using these oils, and mind their powerful scents and the possible reactions they can produce.

The best and quickest way to get results from your oil burner is to place the oils on the burner first, and then light the candle and add hot—not cold!—water. As soon as the hot water makes contact with the oils, you will have an immediate magical connection with the universe.

You can purchase essential oils just about anywhere now; massage therapists, spas, and even supermarkets sell lavender and tea-tree oils. If you're in doubt, the price tag will alert you to an oil's authenticity. Real essential oils aren't cheap, and the bottle is so little that it seems ridiculous to pay so much money for what can seem like a large tablespoon—but don't forget you're getting pure essential oils for your magical needs.

Essential oils on the go

Relaxation
Put three drops of lavender oil in your oil burner.

Finding sleep
Put one drop of jasmine and two drops of clary sage in your oil burner half an hour before bedtime, or sprinkle one drop of clary sage on your pillow one hour before bedtime.

Money

Burn three drops of basil oil in your oil burner for your money needs whenever possible!

Happiness in the home

In your oil burner, place two drops of bergamot and one of neroli for a happy home environment.

Concentration at work

Place two drops of rosemary oil in your handkerchief and smell it every time you feel you need concentration or are about to fall asleep from a lack of motivation.

Homework alertness

Place two drops of peppermint oil and two drops of thyme in your oil burner for alertness and to help your kids concentrate.

Meditation

Place one drop of chamomile oil on your index finger and massage the tips of both of your index fingers together before meditation. Gently rub this oil on your temples.

Attraction

Do I need to say it? Wear rose oil whenever possible!

Protection

Burn in your oil burner two drops of frankincense and one drop of myrrh oil.

If you need a quick protection fix, get an old pot you don't use anymore and fill it up with one liter of water. Bring the water to a boil. Now, take the pot away from the heat and add one crushed garlic clove, two drops of black pepper oil, two drops of frankincense oil, and three drops of rosemary oil. Then take this steaming protection smoke all over the house. Repeat three times, and each time bring the pot back to a boil.

Peace

Always burn lavender oil in your home and at work, in order to drive away disturbances and agitation. Or burn two drops of marjoram to keep the peace.

Magic

Before any magical workings, burn nutmeg oil in your oil burner. Just one drop will do the job.

Aphrodisiac

To enhance sexual drive, burn in your oil burner one drop of vanilla and two drops of patchouli oil.

Keeping your man

Apply one drop of marjoram on his clothes and he will always be yours.

Healing

After an illness, burn sandalwood in your home. Two drops will be enough to bring health back into your world.

Happy essential oils

Bergamot, grapefruit, orange, clary sage, and basil.

De-stress essential oils

Lavender, chamomile, and ylang-ylang.

Protection essential oils

Basil, myrrh, frankincense, rosemary, and garlic.

chapter 8

The Light of a Candle's Flame

I just can't see magic without the flame of a candle! Magic and light go hand in hand, and the flame of a candle is certainly linked to the human spirit. The flame of a candle emits universal energies, and not only do candles bring light for us to be able to see, but they are also a way for us to communicate with the heavens.

The flame of a candle is very powerful. The flame conveys our needs and wants to the universe with strength and sincerity. Candles are my forte. I like to light them when I'm at home—I feel better when I do. Candles keep me focused on a particular intent. Sometimes I have about five candles going all over the house at the same time, and each one is lit for a specific purpose.

My daughter was taking one of her high school exams, and regrettably I wasn't going to be home. I quickly called my mother to ask her to light a yellow candle while visualizing my daughter answering all the questions with confidence and knowledge. My mother was more than willing to do this, knowing that her granddaughter would benefit from a quick fix that only takes a few minutes to do—that is, if you have the right color candle on hand as she did. You can see now why it's so important to keep that "tool stash" fully supplied.

The color of the candles plays a great part in any candle-burning ritual, and just by simply lighting a candle of a certain color you are causing an effect. Each color, as described in chapter 3, has a specific meaning, but instead of *wearing* a specific color, now you're going to use a candle's flame to send your needs to the universe.

I like to dress my candles, no matter if I'm doing a ritual or a quick fix. It doesn't take me long to dress a candle, and if I'm in a hurry, I just take the olive oil bottle from my pantry and splash a little bit on my hand. I then rub my hands together and anoint the candle. My right hand anoints the top of the candle where the wick is, and my left hand does the bottom of the candle. Dressing the candle is just another step in making your needs known to the universe. While you anoint the candle, you're already thinking about your reasons for lighting the candle in the first place, and in turn you are making the universe aware that you're in need.

Once you've finished dressing the candle, light it and then stand in front of it and visualize your needs. Make sure your visualization is clear, without any doubts or negative thoughts. Let your mind take your needs to the universe with sincerity, trust, and love, and trust me—you'll never look back. Magic and light go hand in hand, and both are linked to the human spirit. A candle's flame is mysterious in many ways—as well as beautiful to watch when you are seeking solitude and peace of heart.

Candles on the go

Anger within

For any type of anger, light a light-blue candle in the name of the person who is angry with the world.

Before court day

It's no fun going to court, so light a purple candle and a green candle on a Thursday for good results.

Before meditation

Light a purple candle before any meditation or spiritual workings.

Connection with your spiritual guide

Light a white candle and a purple candle to connect with your spiritual guide.

Concentration and learning

Light yellow candles when your children are doing homework or studying.

Courage for all your needs

Light a red candle and an orange candle on a Tuesday to find the courage you need.

Easing depression

When depression sets in, light a white candle and a pink candle and your depression will diminish.

Ego be gone

If someone has an ego problem, light a green candle and a black candle in that person's name, and his or her ego will subside.

Energy and strength

When you feel you need that get-up-and-go, light a red candle for yourself and you will see.

Enhance a gathering

When you have guest over, light a white candle and a pink candle and a great gathering you will have.

Everyday peace

We all want peace in our homes, and it's always good to have white candles and blue candles burning at all times.

Evil spirits

When there are evil spirits around, light a black candle first and wish them gone. Then light a white candle, and wish the spirits a home that is not yours and is preferably in the heavens above.

Faithful partner

To keep your partner good in all aspects of your relationship, light a green candle and a blue candle on Wednesdays.

Finding a job

Light a green candle and ask the universe to find you the right employment.

Finding love

When you are ready to find the love of your life, light a pink candle and a green candle on Fridays for someone to come along for you to love.

Gaining faith in yourself

When you feel your faith is gone, light a red candle and a white candle to find again the purpose of your soul.

Getting in touch with your angels

To have angels around you, light white candles and purple candles.

Getting rid of hate

When you hate, you block out every single ounce of good energy in your life, so light a black candle and a white candle and wish the hatred that is in your heart gone in order to bring good things back into your life.

Happiness in your life

Always light blue candles for the happiness you need.

Harmony is needed

If it's harmony you need, a blue candle lit first thing in the morning will bring it to you.

Healing friendships

To heal a friendship or to make friends, light a white candle and a blue candle on Wednesdays.

Healing from an illness

To heal from an illness, light a white candle and a blue candle to get you back on track.

Health and well-being

For your health needs, light a white candle and a blue candle. You can also light them in the name of a loved one who needs healing.

In the mood for love

Light a red candle in your bedroom just before bedtime to get you in the mood and ready for an amorous evening.

Love

Light a pink candle and a white candle when you feel you're lacking love in your life.

Luck at every turn

Always have yellow candles at home and light them for good luck.

Money—we all want it and need it

Light green candles whenever possible and send your money needs to the universe as many times as you feel you should.

Moving on after an emotional breakup

After the breakup of a relationship, light a blue candle and a yellow candle. Doing so will enable you to move on, or light the candles in the name of another who needs to move on.

Passionate evening

If passion is needed, light a pink candle and a red candle.

Pregnancy wish

If you are dreaming of becoming a mother, light a yellow candle and a pink candle as much as you like when your timing is right.

Protection against danger

When you feel danger is upon you, light a black candle and a blue candle to ward the danger away from you and the ones you love.

Seeking a promotion

We all want to be promoted, and you will have a better chance if you light a blue candle and a white candle on Thursdays.

Selling your home

Light a green candle every Sunday until your home is sold.

Stop negativity in the home

To get rid of negativity in your home, light a black candle and a white candle every Saturday just before dawn.

Successful business

Light a green candle and an orange candle behind your own business door.

Wanting to be understood

Light an orange candle and a yellow candle when you need the understanding of others.

When help is needed

This is one of my favorites. Light a red candle for your partner to help you around the house.

When in need of protection

Light a black candle and a white candle when you feel that protection is required.

Work environment

To keep your work environment healthy, light a blue candle and a green candle at your place of employment.

Your dream home

Visualizing that you will one day have your own home is great, but lighting a blue candle and a pink candle will reinforce your dreams tenfold. Don't visualize "one day"; instead, visualize owning your home *today*.

Candles for each day of the week

Sunday: Yellow, to aid the healing of the self and to learn something new that day

Monday: White, for purity and protection in your life

Tuesday: Red, for strength and passion all the way

Wednesday: Purple, for wisdom and family communication

Thursday: Blue, for patience and tranquillity during the day

Friday: Green, for growth and love in your life

Saturday: Black, to rid yourself of all the week's negativity and to stay positive for the week ahead

chapter 9

Water and Its Element

The first thing my mother used to tell me to do when I felt sick was to take a shower. "It'll make you feel better," she'd say. Today I tell my own daughter the same thing. Having a shower or a bath has always made me feel 100 percent better, especially when I sense negativity around me. I just get under the shower and wash it all off, and this method always works—with enduring positive results.

Water is associated with the emotions, and emotions are our greatest enemy. If our emotions are out of whack, our physical body will be out of whack as well. Unfortunately, when that happens we can't function and we can't possibly think rationally. The decisions we make in this state are governed solely by our emotional state of mind, and they are often decisions we end up wishing we hadn't made.

The water element is miraculous in its own way. I have always visualized water as a rough sponge and the negativity in our bodies as dirt. Once water touches the body, it becomes more like a tool to scrub away negative energy than anything else—and our positive visualizations become the soap or detergent. The more you visualize, the more cleansing suds you make and the better your chances of getting rid of what's bothering you, whether it be negativity from others or even from yourself.

Now, a bath is an excellent way to utilize the water element. Taking a bath is one of the most relaxing things anyone can do. Moreover, a bath oozes with positive, replenishing energies—energies that your body requires to replace what was taken away throughout the day.

Unfortunately, a bath by itself isn't one of the quick fixes, but using the element of water whenever possible is absolutely essential. If you don't have time for a bath, then try the bucket spells on the go. Okay, don't laugh—the bucket works! These spells are great for those of you who don't have a bathtub in your home or the time to relax in the tub.

Just get yourself a white bucket for your magical water connection with the universe. Once you've added to the bucket what is required by the spell, take the bucket with you and leave it outside the shower with the contents of the spell already in it. Take your shower as you would normally and when you finish, bring the bucket into the shower, fill it up with lukewarm water, and turn off the faucet. Then stand there naked, visualizing your needs to the universe. Place your hand inside the bucket and gently mix the ingredients while visualizing your needs. Once you've finished establishing your needs, hold the bucket up high and pour it over your head, gently letting the water run all over your body.

Once the bucket is empty, don't rinse yourself off. Just step out of the shower and pat yourself dry with a white towel. By doing this, you are sealing yourself and ensuring the bad energy you just got rid of doesn't come back. You're also making sure that the new energy you just put in stays in.

Bucket spells on the go

Wash away stress

In your bucket, place three drops of lavender oil and half a cup of chamomile flowers—and your stress will be a thing of the past.

Wash away negativity

Place in the bucket one teaspoon of cumin powder, a few leaves of fresh basil, and one teaspoon of rock salt. The negativity you hold will be gone.

To attract money

Crush three cooking cloves together with a large cinnamon stick and sesame seeds. Once you've done that, place the mixture in your white bucket. You can do this as many times as you want, and it is best to do it on Thursdays.

After an altercation

Any type of disagreement or fight can leave us in a state of mental and emotional discomfort. To wash away these uncomfortable feelings, place in your white bucket a large tablespoon of salt together with a teaspoon of olive oil.

To attract love

To attract the love you need and want, place in your bucket the petals of a red rose, two drops of spearmint oil, and a bunch of fresh basil.

To stop nasty gossip about you

Fill your bucket with warm-to-hot water. Add in one large tablespoon of sage, one large tablespoon of rosemary, and a bunch of parsley. Let it all sit for about thirty minutes; just before your shower, mix it all together. Once you've finished your shower and the bucket spell, pick up the parsley from the floor of your shower and place it in your garbage can with the gossip.

Before bed

To have a good sleep, place in your bucket three drops of lavender oil and sleep you will find.

For a passionate evening

Place in your bucket all the petals of a fresh red rose, two drops of jasmine oil, and half a teaspoon of olive oil. Mix it all together and over your head it goes. Next, pick up the rose petals and place them inside a dry towel. Pat them dry, then place them under your pillow for the passionate evening you are desperately seeking.

chapter 10

My Family's Spells on the Go

My family and I still do the quick fixes in this chapter when we're in need. My mother has so much information in that little stubborn head of hers that she always surprises me, and the energies here have proved their worth time and time again in our family's magical workings.

I know my Cuban heritage, and we Cubans tend to inflate problems. Conflicts and discord are fed to a frenzy, and guess what happens in my family next . . . well, immediately incense is burned, then out come the herbs, colored cloths, crystals, and candles. Then, to solve the problem, the scent of magic surrounds the room from years of know-how.

Now, in the meantime while all this is happening, my family has not stopped arguing and talking over each other. We are all trying to solve the particular problem that has suddenly arisen for one of the Abrev clan; it's like a war zone! We all want to protect the one who needs protection, and finally we come up with a sensible magical medium and the spell is written, to be done by the one who is in need. But even though we help create spells for each other, we never *do* those spells for the person in need; we each do our own spells, as it has more meaning when you actually get down and visualize your own needs to the universe.

The following few spells are all quick fixes that my family uses and has used with positive results over the years. They are simple and at times strange, but these quick spells have been tested over and over again and shared with others for a particular need. I'm sure you will find something in my family's spells on the go that you can use for your own needs.

My family's spells on the go

Protection from negative entities

When you feel a negative entity is nearby, get a glass of water and splash some cologne inside it. On top of the glass, place a pair of sharp scissors. Light some frankincense incense around your home and also light a white candle. Then, when you are mentally ready, call out to the entity and say, "I'm cutting the energies you feed from and sending you into the light. You must leave me alone and go toward the light."

Spell intention: The water is used to purify the room. The splash of cologne attracts lost entities and acts as a calling note. The frankincense brings protection energies against the entity, and the white candle attracts what is good in them. This spell is best done on a Saturday.

Other quick spells on the go for protection from negative entities:

Place a laurel leaf under your pillow for protection.

Sprinkle ammonia around the house.

Light frankincense or dragon's blood incense.

Light a black candle and a white candle together—the black for the negative entity to go away, and the white for it to go in peace and hope.

Cleansing the body of negative energy

On a Monday, take an egg from your refrigerator and let it sit out all night under the moonlight. On Tuesday morning, go to a place where you can have some privacy—your bathroom will do—and take all your clothes off. Once you're naked, take the egg in your right hand, or left if you are left-handed, and gently rub the egg all over your body. As you do, visualize the negative energy you wish to be rid of. Once you finish, take the egg and break it over your toilet. Let the yolk and egg whites flush down the toilet, and just throw the shell in the garbage can.

Spell intention: My family uses this method to rid ourselves of negative energy—negative energy that someone else has created for us or simply energy that we have created for ourselves.

As you rub the egg over your body, the egg absorbs all the negativity from your body. By flushing the contents of the egg down the toilet, you are flushing that negative energy as far away as you can. The toilet is a means of getting rid of waste, and with this spell you are getting rid of your negative energy waste.

Other quick spells on the go for cleansing the body of negative energy

Have a salt bath, or do a bucket spell with salt.

Light a black candle and blue candle together, and wish the negative energy to go away.

Carry with you a tiger-eye crystal.

Freeze those who do us harm

Fill a clear glass with water. Then, on a small piece of paper, write down the name of the person you know is doing you harm, and tarnishing your reputation, by means of gossip or anger. As you do this, visualize what you would like this person to stop doing, then place the paper with his or her name inside the glass of water. Add one drop of blue food dye, and with a small teaspoon stir together the paper and the food dye in the glass of water. Immediately place the mixture inside your freezer.

Spell intention: The water in the glass makes the connection with the name of the person, and then the blue dye cools off the person you want to stop. By placing the glass inside your freezer, you will freeze any negative intentions toward you.

This spell is one of my favorites, and it works every single time. Do not take this person out of the freezer until you feel his or her negativity has calmed down. If the negativity starts again, do the spell again—but this time add one peppercorn to the water, which will indicate that you mean business.

Other quick spells on the go for those who would do us harm

Light a red candle in the name of the one who is doing you harm, and visualize that person stopping it right *now*.

Carry with you a laurel leaf where no one can see it, or a few pine nuts.

Money

Carry with you phony paper currency—the higher the denomination, the better.

Spell intention: The universe is all about visualizing and staying positive. If you think negatively, you will bring nothing but negative energy, but the more you think in a positive way, the more good things you'll attract. This goes for money, too: the more you have, the more you'll get. Treat your phony paper currency as though it were real, and never, never give it away.

Other quick spells on the go for money

Light a green candle every Thursday.

Carry alfalfa inside your purse or wallet at all times.

Carry with you a cowry shell.

Place cinnamon sticks in decorative bowl and add to the bowl a cup of sesame seeds. Use the bowl as a centerpiece on top of your dinning room table. Refresh it as needed, as long as your money needs last.

Get a large bunch of fresh basil and caress yourself with it from head to toe.

Write yourself a check and don't deposit it—but keep it with you at all times.

Fill a half-shell of a coconut with uncooked rice and place it behind your front door.

Place one drop of patchouli essential oil in your hands in order to take hold of your money needs.

Protection for the home

Find or purchase a clear or white spray bottle, although a blue spray bottle will also do. Once you've got your bottle, place inside it seven rusty nails, seven sewing pins, a tiger-eye crystal, two large tablespoons of rum, and one drop of blue food dye.

Now add water to the bottle, preferably rainwater, and then add four drops of basil essential oil and two large sticks of fresh rosemary leaves. Mix all this together and leave it outside on a full-moon night. Keep the spray bottle and the mixture inside it outside for three more days and three more nights. Let the moon give the bottle its protection strength.

Next, spray the water inside the bottle all over your home on Saturdays to keep your home protected and to magically clean up the negative energy.

Spell intention: In this spell are many protection energies, and once they are mixed together you create a powerful protection liquid that, once it is left under the moonlight and sprayed in your home, will give your home a protection coating that no negativity will be able to penetrate.

Other spells on the go for the protection of your home

Sprinkle ammonia around the house when needed for negativity.

Burn rosemary incense whenever possible to keep negativity away.

Hang a bunch of garlic from the front door.

Behind the front door, keep a red bow.

Place in the four corners of your home four clear quartz crystals, with each of the points facing toward the outside of your residence.

Light blue candles for protection on Tuesdays and Saturdays.

Mix together salt and aloe powder, and sprinkle it around your home.

Always have a clear quartz crystal around your home for protection.

Other family favorites

Protection for your children
Have your child wear an onyx or a tiger-eye crystal.

Visualize a blue light around your child at all times.

Never let your child wear red—instead, he or she should wear yellow or blue for protection.

To help your child after a nightmare
Get your child a stuffed animal. It could be any animal your child can identify with, such as a tiger, a lion, or a bear. If your child has a bad nightmare, tell him or her to hold this stuffed animal and to visualize the toy as a real

animal that will protect against that which has scared your child during the nightmare.

To attract a man
Sew a little red bow on the back of all your underwear.
Have a bucket shower with rose petals.
Carry with you a rose-quartz crystal.

To keep someone happy and on your side
Write the name of the person you wish to have on your side and place the paper on a white plate. Then add honey on top and place the plate up high, where it cannot be seen by anyone. This spell can also be done for a person who needs some sweetening!

For study, research, or concentration
Light a yellow candle.
Burn rosemary oil in your oil burner.
Carry with you a citrine crystal.

To thwart your enemy

On a piece of toilet paper, write the name of the person who has been causing you harm. Flush the toilet paper down the toilet, and whatever your enemy was doing will stop. Now, if you'd like to be more creative with the toilet tissue, please be my guest!

closing

*E*ach living thing possesses an energy field, within and around it, that is filled with earthbound vibrations. When you combine those natural energies with positive thoughts, you generate your wishes and send them to the universe. In spells on the go, you do just that—but without a ritual, so you're able to keep up with the fast pace of modern life.

The more you visualize your needs to the universe, the more the spell will go your way. But if it doesn't, don't despair. There is always a reason, and soon enough you will find out why.

Thank you for letting me share my family's spells and my spells with you. Enjoy them, as they have proved to be very handy in my times of need.

Blessed be,
Ileana

glossary

Astral travel

Separation from the self, an out-of-body experience during which one is aware.

Chakras

The seven light points, and life forces, in our bodies.

Charcoal tablets

A special kind of charcoal that, when lit, can be used to burn herbs and resins.

Dressing a candle

Anointing a candle with specific oils for a particular intent.

Earthbound energies

Energies with life, such as herbs, plants, and crystals.

Essential oils

Oils extracted from flowers, plants, or resins.

Etheric field

The field of pure energy that radiates outside our physical bodies.

Herb

A plant that is valued for its medicinal properties or for its flavor. There are aromatic, culinary, and medicinal herbs.

Magic

The use of natural energies and positive visualization to create change in our lives.

Magical workings

The act of doing and using magic.

New Age store

A shop that sells everything you need for magic, including herbs, crystals, candles, and self-help books that teach spirituality.

Oil burner

A deep, sometimes ceramic, dish with a tea candle on the bottom that is used for burning essential oils.

Santería

A magical practice that originated in Africa.

Talisman

Anything that wards away negative energies and entities.

index